Kindness

Julie Murray

Abdo
CHARACTER EDUCATION
Kids

abdopublishing.com

Published by Abdo Kids, a division of ABDO, PO Box 398166, Minneapolis, Minnesota 55439.

Printed in the United States of America, North Mankato, Minnesota.

052017

092017

THIS BOOK CONTAINS RECYCLED MATERIALS

Photo Credits: iStock, Shutterstock

Production Contributors: Teddy Borth, Jennie Forsberg, Grace Hansen

Design Contributors: Christina Doffing, Candice Keimig, Dorothy Toth

Publisher's Cataloging in Publication Data

Names: Murray, Julie, 1969-, author.

Title: Kindness / by Julie Murray.

Description: Minneapolis, Minnesota : Abdo Kids, 2018 | Series: Character education | Includes bibliographical references and index.

Identifiers: LCCN 2016962329 | ISBN 9781532100109 (lib. bdg.) | ISBN 9781532100796 (ebook) | ISBN 9781532101342 (Read-to-me ebook)

Subjects: LCSH: Kindness--Juvenile literature. | Kindness in children--Juvenile literature. | Children--Conduct of life--Juvenile literature. | Social skills in children--Juvenile literature.

Classification: DDC 179/.9--dc23

LC record available at http://lccn.loc.gov/2016962329

Table of Contents

Kindness 4

More Ways to Be Kind 22

Glossary. 23

Index 24

Abdo Kids Code. 24

Kindness

Kindness is all around.

Do you see it?

Ryan **takes turns** at the water fountain. He is being kind.

Anna reads to her brother.

She is being kind.

Lexi falls down. Ruby helps her get up. She is being kind.

Joel helps his **neighbor** rake.

He is being kind.

Erin brings pink roses to her aunt. She is being kind.

Have you been kind today?

More Ways to Be Kind

donate clothes and toys

hold the door open for someone

pick up litter

tell someone you love them

Glossary

neighbor
a person who lives near another.

take turns
to do something one person after another.

Index

aunt 18

blocks 6

brother 12

fall 14

help 8, 14, 16

neighbor 16

plant 8

read 12

roses 18

share 6

water fountain 10

abdokids.com

Use this code to log on to abdokids.com and access crafts, games, videos, and more!